Monkey

Swing by your arms
With a one-two-three.
Now swing by your legs,
To the top of your tree.
Swing by your tail
And reach with your fingers.
This little monkey
Is the king of the swingers.

Rabbit

Scamper here,
Scamper there,
Rabbits scampering
Everywhere!

Bunny-hop here,
Bunny-hop there,
Rabbits bunny-hopping
Everywhere!

Dig a hole here,
Dig a hole there.
Digging rabbit holes
Everywhere!

Animal Exercises

POEMS to KEEP FIT

by

Mandy Ross

illustrated by

Sanja Rešček

Published by Child's Play (International) Ltd

Swindon   Auburn ME   Sydney

Text © 2006 M...   ...ternational) Ltd

Printed i... Cro...   ...1643-044-5

www.ch...lds-p...   ...1643-044-2

Cheetah

Run! Run!
Who can beat a
Chasing, racing,
Running cheetah?
Nothing neater,
Nothing fleeter,
Speed is beauty
For a cheetah.

Tortoise

Sporty Tortoise?
He's quite a goer.
Does his exercises,
Just a little… slower.

Ready? And…
One step…
Two steps…
Three steps…
Four.

Five steps…
Six steps…
That's enough. No more!

Dolphin

Ocean wide, water cool...
We swim in teams at dolphin school.

One by one,
Over the waves we leap,
Then all together
We dive down deep
To dance in a spiral,
And swim in a ring,
Calling and bleeping –
Together we sing:

Ocean wide, water cool...
Swimming for joy at dolphin school.

Dog

I'm ready to run!
I've found a stick.
Throw! Fetch!
Quicker than quick!

Past the trees,
Along the track,
Fast as the wind,
And bring it back.

Ready to run!
Here's the stick.
Throw it again?
Quicker than quick!

Ant

Hup two three four five six!
Hup two three four five six!
One by one in a long line walking,
One by one, no time for talking.
Hup two three four five six!
Hup two three four five six!
Work, work, work, we work all day,
Work, work, work, no time to play.
Hup two three four five six!
Hup two three four five six!

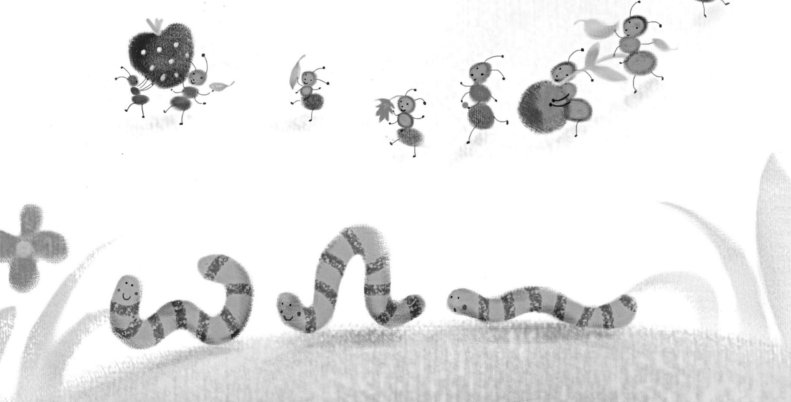

Worm

Bend and stretch, and stretch and bend.
Wiggle in the middle, and wave each end.
Now squirm and squiggle, and squiggle and squirm,
You're a wiggly, squiggly, healthy worm!

Bird

Flying exercises.
Are you ready?
Perched for take-off;
Hold it steady...
Don't look down –
Aim for the sky.
Flap those wings!
You're off! You can fly!

Kangaroo

Long jump, high jump,
Just-passing-by jump.

Quick jump, slow jump,
Long-way-to-go jump.

Big jump, small jump,
Faster-than-you-all jump.

Morning-till-night jump
Then sleep-till-it's-light jump.

Squirrel

Instructions:
Sing the song below while doing these squirrel exercises:
1. Find a nut   *4. Remember where you buried it*
2. Dig a little hole   *5. Can't find it?*
3. Bury your nut   *6. Repeat from (1)*
You will soon be as fit as a squirrel.

I'll dig a little hole
For a conker or a nut.
I'll remember where I put it,
I'm sure I will...but...

Digging here beneath this tree,
Searching for a nut.
I thought I left one buried here.
I'm sure I did...but...

I'll dig another little hole
For just another little nut.
I'll remember where I put it,
I'm sure I will...but...

Digging here beneath this tree,
Searching for a nut.
I thought I left one buried here.
I'm sure I did...but...

Lemur

We run along the branches,
Babies on our backs.
Up and down the tree trunks,
Never leaving tracks.
Stripy tails a-balancing,
Turning left and right,
Leaping high from tree to tree –
Keep holding tight!

Hippo

Oversize?
Don't agonize.
Just make sure
You exercise.
Large behind?
Never mind!
Jump in the river,
And soon, you'll find
You're feeling slim,
And looking trim.
Who needs the gym?
Just splash and swim.

Meerkat

Standing still, alert,
Straight and tall,
Keeping watch
You'll see us all.

On our marks,
Heads held high.
At the slightest danger,
Get set... Goodbye!

Donkey

You put your right hooves in,
You put your right hooves out,
In, out, in, out,
You shake them all about.
You do the donkey-cokey
And you turn around,
And that's what it's all about.

Oh, oh, oh the donkey-cokey!
Oh, oh, oh the donkey-cokey!
Oh, oh, oh the donkey-cokey!
Knees bend, tail stretch,
Hee-haw-haw!

Verse 2: You put your left hooves in...
Verse 3: You put your tail in...
Verse 4: You put your whole self in...

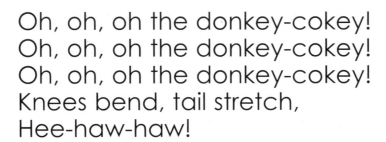

Pig

We're nice and plump here in our sty.
Oink! Oink! I'll whisper why…
We like fat bottoms and fat thighs –
We don't believe in exercise.

Plump and peachy, pink and plump,
We never run or leap or jump.
We never jump or run or leap,
Just sleep and eat, then eat and sleep.

Lizard

Start... scuttle...
Stop!

Scuttle, scuttle, scuttling...
And...
Stop!

Start...
Scuttle, scuttle, scuttling...
Over the rocks we run.
We scuttle, then we stop...
To bask in the sun.

Start...

Stop!

We bask in the sun
Very still, not a wink,
And when the sun goes down,
We scuttle home in a blink.

Scuttle...
Stop!

Scuttle, scuttle, scuttle home...
And stop!

Snail

Line up for the snail race,
Ready, steady, go.
Off at a snail's pace –
Very, VERY slow.
Don't go quickly,
Don't go fast.
Who's the winner?
The one who comes last!

slug

Now for the slug race,
Also VERY slow.
Off at a slug's pace,
Watch them go!
Racing to the lettuce patch
In time for lunch.
Prizes for everyone:
Fresh leaves to munch!

Rhinoceros

Eleven rhinoceri
In our team,
Hooves a-polished,
Horns a-gleam.

We're large and lumbering,
We aren't very quick,
But we're fab at football
Just watch us kick!
'Up the Rhinoceri!'
Hear the crowd roar.
We pass... we dribble...
We shoot... we score!

Octopus

Wiggle those tentacles,
S-t-r-e-t-c-h them out.
Roll them all up,
Then shake them all about.

Fish

Every little fishy ought
To do their best at fishy sport.
Backstroke, sidestroke, fishstroke, crawl;
Little fishies learn them all.
Now, under the waves and out to sea –
Race you back in time for tea.

Starfish

Most fish
Can't jump,
But starfish
Starjump.

Cat

You'll never see an acrobat
More graceful than a balancing cat.
Along the fence, along the wall,
We never stumble, never fall.
Toes pointed, tail held high,
Nose in the air as we pass by.
Leaping lightly down from the wall,
We land on our feet, we never fall.

Mouse

Running on tiptoe,
Quiet as a mouse,
Upstairs, downstairs,
All around the house.

Running on tiptoe,
Quiet as a mouse.
Tiny furry exercises,
All around the house.

Elephant

Four steps left and four steps right,
Keep those elephant footsteps light.
Twirl to the left, yes, that's the knack,
Now four steps right and four steps back.

Take your partner by the trunk,
Swing to the right and bump your rump.
Round to the left and form an arch,
Then two-by-two right through you march.

Oh! Twirl to the left, yes, that's the knack,
Four steps right and four steps back.
Now four steps left and four steps right,
And keep those elephant footsteps light!

Tree frog

Frogs like leapfrog,
We love to leap.
We're always leaping
(Unless we're asleep).
I leap over you,
Then you leap over me.
Frogs like leapfrog,
As anyone can see!

Sloth

This you wake me up to ask?
Did I hear you right?
The best exercise? For sloths?
Yaww-ww-n! Good night!
Zzzzzzzzzzz......

Bat

Join the stars like dot-to-dot,
We bats go flitting by.
Race you to the moon and back,
Chase you through the midnight sky.

Owl

Exercise should only be taken after dark,
In the heart of the forest, or deep in the park.
Take care with your swooping
And looping the looping.
Night flying exercise,
Wide wings sweeping,
Circling the darkness
While the other world's sleeping.

Swoop and whoop
And swoop the loop.
Loop and swoop,
To-whit, to-whoop!

Swoop and whoop and swoop the loop! Loop and swoop, to-whit, to-whoop!
Swoop and whoop and swoop the loop! Loop and swoop, to-whit, to-whoop!

Human

Can you run on tiptoe, quiet as a mouse?
Dance like an elephant all around the house?
Swoop like an owl, leap like a frog,
Jump like a starfish, chase like a dog?
Hop like a bunny, or a kangaroo, or both?
Phew! Enough exercise! Now sleep like a sloth.